He walked to the line.

He couldn't help thinking back to the last time he had come to the line with a game to win or lose.

And now the shouting had gone crazy.

His own fans were cheering for him, telling him he could do it. But the Bulls were going crazy. "Choke, choke," some of them were chanting. "Choke like you did before."

But Miles smiled. This was going to be sweet. He knew he wouldn't miss this time.

Catch the action with the
Angel Park Hoop Stars!

ANGEL PARK HOOP STARS

4

ON THE LINE

By Dean Hughes

Illustrated by Dennis Lyall

Bullseye Books • Alfred A. Knopf
New York

Library of Congress Cataloging-in-Publication Data
Hughes, Dean, 1943–
On the line / by Dean Hughes ; illustrated by Dennis Lyall.
p.   cm. — (Angel Park hoop stars ; vol. 4)
Summary: Unless star guard Miles "Tip" Harris can keep his cool
under pressure from opposing players, the Angel Park Lakers could
have a short season.
ISBN 0-679-83490-7 (pbk.) — ISBN 0-679-93490-1 (lib. bdg.)
[1. Basketball—Fiction.] I. Lyall, Dennis, ill. II. Title. III. Series:
Hughes, Dean, 1943–   Angel Park hoop stars ; vol. 4.
PZ7.H87312On   1993   [Fic]—dc20   92-13788

First Bullseye Books edition: February 1993

Manufactured in the United States of America

to Bobby Callahan

★1★

Hot Shooter

Miles "Tip" Harris took a quick pass from his point guard, Jackie Willis. He turned and faced the basket. Denny Korman, the lanky forward for the San Lorenzo Suns, was staring him straight in the face.

Miles faked a move forward and then stepped back. He fired a jump shot.

Rip!

The shot split the net.

And the Lakers were off to a 2 to 0 lead.

All the players on the Lakers' bench hooted and hollered, and Miles felt good. He had the touch today. He could feel it.

The Suns better look out!

Miles hurried back on defense. The Lakers were using a box-and-one zone. Four players covered the key area in a square formation. Kenny Sandoval was out front, staying toe to toe with Justin Smagler, the Suns' point guard and best shooter.

Kenny shuffled backward down the floor with Smagler. He made the guy work just to get the ball across the time line.

Smagler was getting frustrated. He finally tried to throw a long pass to Korman. But Miles dashed in and caught the ball on the run. He darted for the other end of the floor.

Smagler tried to cut off his path to the hoop, but Miles drove hard.

He leaped for the lay-up.

Smagler jumped high for the block.

But Miles hesitated in the air. He held off on the shot until Smagler was coming down. Then he flipped the ball up and in.

The whole crowd gasped.

No one else in the league could have made that shot. Miles, a sixth grader, had the body control of someone twice his age. He was fairly tall for his age, and built well. He was also one of the two black players on the team.

"Way to go, Tip," Jackie yelled. Jackie was the other black player. She was fairly small but quick, and a great ball handler. And she played *hard*.

The Lakers got tough on defense again.

This time, Sullivan, the Suns' other guard, took a pass from Smagler but couldn't find anyone open. Finally, he blasted away at the basket, but the shot was short.

Harlan Sloan, the Lakers' tall center, gathered in the rebound as it came off the front of the rim. He hit Jackie with a bullet pass. She dribbled quickly up the court.

The Suns got back in a hurry, and they stopped the fast break. But Jackie spotted Miles as he broke past Korman toward the hoop. She looped the ball high—an alley-oop pass.

Miles leaped toward the basket and caught the ball. And in the same motion, he laid it off the glass.

Score!

Six to nothing, and the game had hardly started.

The Lakers' subs—and all the parents and fans—were really whooping it up.

Miles felt as though he could fly. No one would stop him today!

But the Suns' coach called time out. Clearly, he wanted to talk things over with his team before it was too late.

Coach Donaldson gathered his team in a circle. Then he told them, "All right. Great start. My guess is, they'll come back with two of their kids guarding Harris. So we've got to get the ball to some other people."

Miles nodded.

He hated to think that he wouldn't get many chances to shoot for a while. But he also thought that the coach's plan was right.

The teams walked back to the floor.

As Miles took up his defensive position, Korman walked over to him. "You think you're a real hotshot, don't you, Harris?" he said. He bumped Miles's shoulder with his chest.

Miles didn't back away, but he also didn't say anything. He knew better than to start jawing with the guy. He had learned a long time ago that the way to put down a mouthy kid like that was to outplay him.

"You came from LA thinking none of us could play ball out here, didn't you?"

Miles had heard this sort of thing before in Angel Park. He just tried not to listen.

The Suns tossed the ball inbounds. Play was back in action.

"Don't try any of your cute stuff on me, or I'll put you on your butt, LA boy."

Miles glanced at him this time. He almost said something, but he held back.

But he played Korman really tight. He kept him from getting free for a pass.

Smagler, however, slipped by Kenny and got a pass from Klein, the tall center.

Smagler was in the clear, and he popped in a jumper from the side of the lane.

Korman ran down the floor, shoulder to shoulder with Miles. He bumped him a couple of times, and Miles knew it was on purpose.

"If you think you're going to get the ball, you're crazy," he told Miles.

Miles kept telling himself not to let this guy bother him. But he was *very* happy when he saw that the coach's guess had been wrong. Miles wasn't double-teamed.

The Suns' coach must have told Korman

to get on Miles tight and keep the ball out of his hands.

But *no way* could he stop Miles by himself.

Miles loped all the way to the corner. He watched Jackie bring the ball to the top of the key.

He made a move toward the baseline, forcing Korman back. Then—suddenly—he cut to his left and ran toward Jackie.

She saw Miles get open and she passed him the ball. But she didn't hit him as quickly as she might have. Korman caught up.

Tip thought of passing off, but he knew he was hot. And he wanted to shut Korman's mouth.

He spun, faked, and then went up for the jump shot.

Korman leaped straight up, with his hands in front of Miles's face.

And the shot was off line.

Klein beat Harlan to the rebound. Then he passed to Smagler.

The Suns hustled back up the court, and this time Kenny tried a little too hard to stop

Smagler. He fouled him in the act of shoot-ing.

Smagler hit only one of the foul shots, but the six-point lead was already cut in half.

Miles was mad at himself. He knew he hadn't taken a good shot. He should have looked for an open player and passed off.

And Korman was loving it. "Hey, hotshot, that was a pretty weak shot. You gotta do better than that."

Miles told himself to be cool—to play smart.

The next time he got the ball, he spotted Harlan open at the foul line. He shot a quick pass to him.

Harlan made a good move to the hoop, but the lay-up rolled off the rim and the Suns got the rebound.

"What's the matter, Harris, afraid to shoot against me now? Afraid I'll make you look bad?"

"Shut up, will you?" Miles finally barked back at him.

"Oh, oh. What's the matter? Is the hotshot getting mad? I thought you LA boys had more cool than that."

"I told you to shut up!" Miles yelled at Korman.

All this happened while they were running down the floor. And Miles soon knew that the coach had been watching.

He saw Ben Riddle take his warmups off and go to the scorer's table. The next time the action stopped, Ben ran straight to Miles. "I'm in for you," he said.

Korman walked away, but he shot back a glance at Miles. He looked very pleased with himself.

Miles trotted to the sideline. Now he knew he was really in for it.

The coach was standing up, waiting for him. "Okay, I know," Miles said, before the coach could say a word. "But you ought to hear the stuff that guy is saying to me."

"I don't care what he says. You don't say *one thing* back to him. Do you understand that?"

"Yeah. Sure."

But the problem was, Miles got no chance for a while. The coach left him on the bench for the rest of the quarter.

And things weren't going well. Ben tried hard, but he wasn't half the player Miles was.

The Suns were rolling now. By the end of the quarter, they had moved ahead, 13 to 10.

When Miles got back in the game, he had talked to himself plenty. No way was he going to let Korman bother him. He would just play his game.

But the guy started in again. "Hey, are *you* back? That other kid's a better player. I don't know why your coach wants you out here."

Miles walked away from Korman, pretending not to hear. But the first chance he got, he burst away from Korman and got a pass.

He was wide open. He spun and pumped up a fifteen-foot shot. It rattled the rim but rolled out.

Josh fought for the rebound. Then he went back up, hard, and he got the basket.

But Korman was laughing. "You've lost your touch, Harris. You're thinking too much about *me*."

For on instant, Miles almost spun toward the guy. What he wanted to do was smack him in the face.

But he didn't do it. He took a deep breath

and told himself not to get himself thrown out of the game. He would show Korman yet.

The next time he got the ball, he was tempted to shoot, but he saw Harlan break to the hoop. He hit him with a perfect bounce pass, and Harlan got the lay-up.

Miles was pleased with himself. He had done the right thing.

But there was Korman, at his side. "Afraid to shoot now, Mr. LA?"

And suddenly Miles made up his mind. He was going to make this guy look sick.

Sullivan tried to drive the lane. Harlan cut him off, and Sullivan couldn't find anyone to pass to.

Three seconds in the lane.

The ball went over to the Lakers.

Miles stayed back with the guards. He ran alongside Jackie as she brought the ball into forecourt. And then he called out, "Here, Jackie. Give me the ball."

Jackie passed to him, and Miles drove straight at Korman.

Korman took him on, but Miles dribbled behind his back, cut to the left and made Korman look silly.

Miles was open, driving to the hoop. But he was pushing hard—maybe too hard. As he leaped for the lay-up, somehow he lost control of the ball.

It slipped out of his hands and flew out of bounds.

Korman didn't say much. He had looked too bad on the play. But the Suns' whole bench was getting in the act now. "Hey, Harris, what's the problem?"

"What's the matter, *gunner*? You losing your touch?"

Miles ran by the bench. He couldn't resist. "Just wait," he shouted. "I'll *show* you guys what I can do!"

But Coach Donaldson didn't like that at all.

A few seconds later, Miles was heading for the bench again.

★2★

Hot Coach

━━━━━━━━━━━━━━━━━━━━━━━━━━━━

Miles went back in the game after a couple of minutes. But his shooting touch was *gone*.

By halftime, the Suns were ahead 27 to 20.

And the coach was hot.

"Harris, what was going on out there?" he shouted.

"That Korman guy was on my back. He kept telling me—"

"I don't care what he was saying. I can't believe you let that kid get to you like that. You were forcing up shots you had no business taking."

"I know."

"Well, start playing your own game. You don't have to prove *anything* to *anyone*. That kid isn't good enough to stay on the same court with you."

Coach Donaldson was being his usual grouchy self—but Miles sort of liked what he had said. It was, after all, a compliment.

Tip made up his mind to relax and play. He would let Korman talk all he wanted to.

"I don't think I have to remind you," Coach Donaldson said. "This could be the championship game."

Miles was thinking the same thing.

The coach stood, silent, with his hands on his hips. Then he rubbed a hand over his crew-cut hair. "We have two losses—so do the Bulls. We lose this one, and we may be dead. The Bulls have a good chance of going undefeated the rest of the way."

Miles knew that, too. This game mattered too much to let some smart mouth mess him up.

When Miles walked back to the court, his dad was waiting for him. "Look, son," he said, "I could see what that kid was doing to you. But you can't let him get away with it. Just play your game, and don't let him bother you."

"I know, Dad. That's what I'm going to do."

And he did.

When Miles got ready to play, Korman started in again. But Miles said, "You played some good defense in the first half. You guys have a good team."

Korman was caught off guard. He couldn't think of a thing to say.

In fact, Miles scored six points before Korman seemed to get his tongue back.

But Miles was back in the groove. The whole team was playing better. By the end of the third quarter, the score was 41 to 39. The Suns' lead was down to two.

The Lakers tossed the ball in to start the final quarter. Jackie dribbled to the forecourt, and then she passed to Miles on the right side.

Miles made a sudden move, as though he were breaking for the basket. Korman broke with him. But Miles stopped just as suddenly. He stepped back behind the three-point line and let go with a rainbow shot that *slashed* the net.

Three points, and the Lakers had the lead, 42 to 41.

Korman was frustrated by now, and his smart remarks were starting to sound stupid. "Now you *really* think you're hot, don't you? Well, don't think you can keep doing that."

But Miles soon got another chance.

Next time on offense, Jackie passed to Kenny. Kenny cut across the center and set a pick for Josh. Harlan got the ball to Josh in the open, and he took the shot.

The shot was a little long, however, and it bounced high off the rim.

But Miles was there.

He leaped high, caught the ball with one hand, and pushed it back up.

It bounced off the backboard and through the basket.

"That's our *tip*-man," Derek Mahana yelled from the bench.

Miles loved it. He got a high five from Harlan. He hustled back up the floor.

Korman ran alongside Miles, and he mumbled, low and mean. "You think you're a big *star*, don't you, Harris?"

Miles pulled up and took his defensive position.

But Korman looked Miles in the face. "You guys *all* think you're hot. But we don't think so out here. You should have stayed in LA."

Miles knew what Korman meant. He wasn't just talking about basketball anymore.

But Miles didn't react.

Be cool, he told himself. This guy is just one *jerk*. I don't have to let him get to me. All he would have to do is fly off the handle, just once, and everyone—all the white players and their parents—would be talking about the black kid with the bad temper.

The Suns' bench was working on Miles too.

Miles didn't pay any attention to the words. He heard something worse. Maybe it was just jealousy, but it sounded more like hate.

Why didn't their coach stop them?

He tried to concentrate on defense.

Smagler broke loose for a drive down the middle. Then he shoveled the ball off to Korman.

Korman put a shoulder down and tried to drive past Miles. Miles did a good job of cutting off his path, but Korman bulled ahead anyway, right into Miles.

Miles went down, knocked on his backside. And Korman laid the ball up and in.

Miles couldn't believe it. He scrambled to his feet. "That was a foul!" he shouted to the referee. But the ref paid no attention, and to Miles it seemed that everyone was against him.

The Suns' bench only took the opportunity to pour on the smart stuff.

"What's the matter, Harris? Afraid of a little contact?"

"Hey, if you're afraid to play, go sit down!"

And somewhere in the jumble of words, he heard, "That's how those guys are."

Miles couldn't believe what he was hearing. Be cool, he told himself again. Just be cool.

He knew the Suns weren't going to let up now. They were really trying to get to him.

When Miles got a pass along the sidelines, all of the Suns' bench players screamed, "Shoot, *gunner!* Shoot! Shoot!"

Miles dribbled along the baseline and bounced a pass to Brett Sanders, who was in the game for Harlan.

Brett should have had an easy lay-up, but he never quite got hold of the ball. Klein got a hand on it and knocked it away.

All the way up the court, the Suns' bench was working on Miles again. "Afraid to shoot, Harris?" they were shouting.

Korman was saying the same thing.

It was stupid. They had been calling him a "gunner" just a few seconds before.

Miles knew what they wanted to say. Why didn't they just come out and say it? And why didn't some of his own teammates—or even Coach Donaldson—try to put a stop to all this?

But the Suns wouldn't stop, and Miles was struggling to keep control.

The game stayed close.

Jackie got free for a shot that gave the Lakers a three-point lead. But then Klein drove the lane, put in the basket, and got fouled by Brett Sanders.

Klein canned the foul shot, and the game was tied.

With less than three minutes to go, the coach sent Harlan back in the game. It was gut-check time—time to put this game away.

Miles had a deep sense that when the chips were down, he was the guy who could get it done. He shut out all the screaming and yelling, and he went to work.

He cut away from Korman and got free for a pass. He drove straight at the basket, pulled in the defense, and then fired a perfect pass to Josh.

Josh hit a short jumper off the glass, and the Lakers were up by two.

Miles was finally shutting out all the stuff coming from Korman and the Suns' bench. He wanted this victory.

He got on Korman, tight, and watched for a chance to crash the board for a rebound.

Klein took a pass at the foul line. He spun and shot, with Harlan right on him. The shot missed, but the whistle sounded.

Foul on Harlan.

Klein hit the first shot but missed the second.

The score was 48 to 47. The Lakers still had the lead.

Jackie came back with a great move. She cut off Harlan, got the pass on a give-and-go, and laid the ball up and . . .

But the ball rolled off the rim and Klein grabbed the rebound.

Back came the Suns. This time Korman got the ball and tried to drive past Miles.

Miles held his ground, but Korman pulled up and tried to get off a jump shot.

The whistle sounded, and Miles knew the truth. He had gotten a hand on the ball, but he had also slammed Korman across the arm.

Korman went to the line.

Miles didn't say a word, but he was mad at himself.

Still, Miles knew that Korman didn't have much touch—especially with the pressure on.

Sure enough, Korman banged the ball off the front of the rim on the first shot.

He hit the rim with the second shot, too, but he got a good bounce, and the ball dropped in.

Miles knew he had to make something happen. Time was running down fast. The Lakers *had* to score this time down the floor.

Miles ran hard to take up his offensive position. When Jackie dribbled the ball across the line, Smagler was on her close. She passed off to Kenny.

Kenny dribbled to the right and looked for Miles. But Sullivan and Korman were doubling on him.

Kenny used the chance to drive toward the hoop. He drew Sullivan away from Miles.

The idea was right, but when Kenny bogged down in the middle, he tried to loop a pass out to Miles. Korman jumped high and knocked the ball away.

Smagler was right there. He grabbed the ball and raced up the floor.

Jackie went after him, and she made up some ground. But she couldn't get there in time, and Smagler got the basket.

The Lakers were in trouble!

Jackie jumped out of bounds with the ball, and Miles charged toward her. She tossed the ball to him, and he spun and charged up the court. He knew that only a few seconds were left.

The Lakers were down by two. This was it.

Miles dribbled straight for the basket.

When Sullivan tried to block the way, Miles put a spin move on him and went for the hoop. Klein was there, ready to reject the shot. But Miles saw that coming and fed the ball to Josh, who was breaking to the hoop.

It all worked perfectly, except that the whistle sounded. As Josh laid the ball in, the ref shouted, "No basket."

The ref had already called Klein with a

foul for hacking Miles as he had passed off.

So the game was on the line.

Miles had to make both foul shots.

He looked up at the clock and saw that only two seconds remained in the game. If he could put the shots down, he could get the game to overtime.

Miles loved it. He was an excellent foul shooter. He liked nothing better than to come through when he had to.

The Suns' fans were screaming like crazy people. Miles heard the noise, but not the words.

He took very little time. He stepped to the line, eyed the basket, and fired. He watched the ball snap the net.

He bounced the ball a couple of times and got ready for the second shot. The noise all started again.

But just as he was ready to shoot, words came through the noise. And the words jarred him. The moment he released the shot, he knew it was off line.

The ball rattled the hoop and then popped out.

The Suns had won, 50 to 49.

Tough Mind

Miles didn't want to talk to anyone after the game. He rode home with his parents. Both of them kept telling him that the loss wasn't his fault. They were both very upset about the things Miles had put up with—and that no one had put a stop to it.

But Miles knew he had let those guys get to him—and so they had won.

He sat in the back seat and stared out the window. And when he got home, he went to his bedroom and got his basketball.

Then he walked outside to the hoop in his driveway. He stood at the foul line he had marked, and he shot foul shots.

He hardly ever missed.

After Miles had been out there for a while, his dad came out the back door. "It's cold out here," he said. He tucked his hands in his pockets. He didn't have a jacket on.

Miles didn't say anything.

"I see you're shooting foul shots," Dad said.

Miles nodded.

"Have you made them all so far?"

"No."

"Nobody does."

Miles nodded again. He was ready to admit that was true. He had been thinking about it.

"You know, Miles, you're the guy your team goes to in the crunch. That's a compliment to you. But sometimes the shots just aren't going to fall."

Mr. Harris stepped closer and took the basketball from Miles. He rolled it around in his hands. He turned and took a look at the hoop, and then he fired up a shot.

His motion was smooth, but the shot rimmed out of the basket.

"See. Nobody makes them all. Not even me. And I'm a *great* player." He smiled.

Miles chased the ball down. When he turned around, he said, "It wasn't the foul shot that lost the game. It was the way I played before that—in the first half. I lost my cool."

"That's right. And I'll tell you why they want to ride you like that. They can't beat you any other way. So they have to mess with your mind."

"I know."

"If you're going to be really good at this game, you can't let that stuff bother you. Once kids know they can beat you that way, they'll never let up."

Miles nodded. "I know," he said again. It was all the stuff he had been thinking.

"Well, you learned something today." Mr. Harris patted Miles on the shoulder, and then he started to walk away.

"Dad?"

"Yeah."

"Some of that stuff they were saying was because I'm black."

Dad stopped and turned around. He took a long breath, and then he looked Miles straight on. "I hate to say it, son, but I'm sure that's true. I guess that shouldn't surprise us too much, though."

"Maybe it's stuff kids think—but no one ever said it before."

"What did they say to you?"

"That Korman guy started saying, 'You guys' are all this way or that way. Then, just before I took that shot, guys were yelling, 'Go back to LA,' and everything like that. I was doing okay at shutting it out. But then one of them yelled, 'Go back to the *jungle*.' "

Mr. Harris stiffened, and Miles saw the anger flash in his eyes. But he took a long breath, and he said, rather calmly, "I didn't hear that. But I'm not surprised. San Lorenzo is a little town. I doubt that any black people even live there. I'm sure there's plenty of prejudice in a place like that."

"It's here in Angel Park, too, Dad."

"I know. But remember, a lot of kids have been really nice to you, and a lot of them are white." He stepped forward and put a hand on Miles's shoulder. "Son, I wish all this stuff didn't happen. I wish you didn't have to go through any of it."

Miles looked down. He bounced his basketball a couple of times. He wished that he could just be angry.

He didn't want to hurt, too.

"In some ways, you've got it tougher than I had it when I was a kid. At least we knew how we stood with whites in those days. Now, a lot of people put on an act like everything has changed, but too many of them are just hiding the way they really feel."

"If some guy doesn't like me, that isn't so hard to take," Miles said. "I just say, 'Forget him.' But it's the way kids *think* about me that I get sick of."

"Like what?"

"Everyone has the idea that if you're black, you *should* be good at basketball. They don't give you any credit. I practice more than any kid in this whole league. I *know* I do. If I'm any good, it's because I've worked at it."

"You and I both know that, Miles." Mr. Harris slid his hands into his pockets again, and he shivered a little. He was wearing a baggy old pair of pants that he like to wear on Saturdays. He was a tall man. But he didn't play sports anymore, and he had gotten a little thick around the middle.

"It's not just the players, either. It's Coach Donaldson, too. He says he doesn't like my *style of play*. But I think there's more to it than that. I don't think he likes blacks."

"How do you know?"

"He didn't say one thing about all that stuff kids were saying to me. And all he can talk about is the way I play 'street ball.' And why hasn't he been fair with Jackie? He only let her play after she proved about ten times that she was better than Tommy. He even admitted he didn't like to have girls on the team. But I think it's also because she's black."

"Well, maybe. I don't know, Miles. But I think he's coming around. You and Jackie are showing him some things. He's showing you more respect all the time. You have to give *him* a fair chance, too."

Miles shrugged. "It doesn't matter now, anyway," he said. "The season is over."

"Maybe. Maybe not." He put his hand back on Miles's shoulder. "But you have to be tough—*mentally tough*—the rest of the way. Maybe you can't shut out all the stuff they yell at you, but you can't let them break you. Just think of all the abuse a guy like Jackie Robinson put up with. But he held his head up, and he played his game—and he changed the world in a lot of ways."

"I know." But Miles knew that was easier said than done.

"Miles, it's not just basketball. It's life. You're always going to meet up with people like that—people who make up their minds about you before they even know you. There are ways to fight them, and that's something we have to do. But when you sink to their level, you lose. When you rise above it, you win."

Miles turned and fired up a shot.

It swished the net.

Dad grinned and gave him a high five. "You're good, Miles," he said. "Really good. Better than I was at your age. You're going to do some big stuff in your life. Don't let the people with little minds get to you, all right?"

"All right."

Miles felt a lot better after that. Or at least he did until practice on Monday afternoon.

Coach Donaldson thought it was time for another one of his speeches.

He paced back and forth in front of the players. They were sitting in a line. He was wearing his usual gray sweats, and he was talking like *the boss*—as usual.

"Let's face it. The championship may be gone. The Bulls still have to play the Warriors. If the Warriors can beat them, we're back in the picture. Otherwise, we blew it on Saturday."

Miles noticed that the coach was looking right at him.

But the first person he criticized was Jackie.

"Willis, you can't keep trying to get the ball to Harris all the time. We have five players out there."

After that, he had something to say to everyone. But he saved his real anger for last.

"And Harris, I was starting to think you

had a head for this game. But those smart alecks from San Lorenzo went to work on you, and you fell right into their hands."

Miles nodded. He didn't dare say anything, but he wanted to let the coach know that he already realized that.

That didn't stop Coach Donaldson.

"They rode you pretty hard, but what did you do? You decided you would show them. So you had to start hotdogging with the ball—taking shots you had no business taking."

Miles knew that he had done that early in the game. But he had cut it out in the second half. Hadn't the coach noticed that?

"You grew up playing street ball, and when the chips are down, you go back to it."

Miles's muscles suddenly locked. He fought back the desire to react.

"As soon as some kid challenges you, you think you have to show him up. Well, the way to show him up, is to hit the open man—

not to start thinking you have to score all the points yourself."

Miles still didn't say anything. But he was sick of this. Just let this season end, he told himself.

But Harlan finally spoke up. "Coach, those San Lorenzo guys were yelling some bad stuff. Racial stuff."

"Oh, come on, Sloan!" the coach barked. "That's an easy excuse. Those kids don't care what color Harris is."

The gym was suddenly very silent.

Coach Donaldson looked at Miles. "You're not using *that* as an excuse, are you?"

"I'm not using *anything* as an excuse," Miles hissed back at him.

"I sure hope not. If those guys think they can say something to you—anything—and get you to fall apart, then they'll keep right on using it. You've got to be ready for that stuff—and just ignore it."

Yeah, right, Miles thought. Just like I ignored what you told me about playing "street ball."

Miles was mad enough to explode. But that would give Coach Donaldson too much satisfaction—the same as those San Lorenzo guys.

So Miles kept his mouth shut. He would just let the season come to an end—and hope for a better coach next year.

★ 4 ★

Clipping Along

On Saturday, the Lakers played the Cactus Hills Clippers. And the Clippers were not a great team. But another loss and all chance for a championship would be gone.

So the Lakers felt some pressure.

Coach Donaldson didn't help. He poured it on before the game. "You didn't use your heads last week," he told them. "If you play like that today, this Cactus Hills bunch will sneak up and get you. They've got a couple of guards who can shoot the ball."

And that was true. The Clippers didn't have any big players, but they had Zach

Harrison and Chase Higdon, who were both good shooters and ball handlers.

They also had a girl named Sandy LeDuc, who was starting for them now at forward. She was way too short to be much of a rebounder. But if you let her get open, she could shoot from outside.

Miles didn't believe for a minute that the Clippers could knock off the Lakers. Still, he made up his mind that he wouldn't "force" any shots.

He would make his cuts, set his screens—be part of the offense. If he got a clear shot, he would take it. But he wasn't going to take any more chewing out for shooting too much.

In the first quarter, however, the Lakers didn't look sharp. They ran their plays, and they got their shots. But no one was hitting, including Miles.

The Lakers stayed ahead, but that was mainly because Harlan and Josh and Miles kept getting the rebounds off their own missed shots.

Sometimes they were getting three and four shots before they would finally get the ball in the hole.

With their big height advantage, they should have been running away with the game. But they kept fumbling the ball away or staying in the paint too long—all kinds of mental mistakes.

At the end of the quarter, the score was 9 to 6.

Coach Donaldson almost screamed at them. "I was afraid of this. You thought all you had to do was show up and this team would drop over and let you run all over them."

What he didn't mention was that the Lakers had worked hard on defense. They had stayed tough on the guards, playing man-to-man, and they hadn't let them get many clear shots.

In the second quarter, the coach put Tommy and Derek in the game at the guard positions. They didn't stay with Harrison and Higdon nearly as well.

Harrison got hot, and he knocked down two jumpers and a long three-pointer. The coach hustled Jackie back into the game, but by then the Clippers were starting to believe they could make a game of it.

Higdon hit a couple of outside shots. And LeDuc got another one over Josh.

At least the Lakers were starting to play better offense themselves.

Harlan was tough inside against the smaller center. Jackie was getting the ball to him, and he was driving for lay-ups. Or he passed to the forwards if the defense pulled in on him.

The score stayed close. The Lakers lost the lead for a while, but they got it back. With a minute and a half to go in the half, the score was 23 to 22.

The Cactus Hills kids were not a bunch of smart mouths. They hadn't said anything to Miles. So nothing like that was bothering him.

But something was.

He still wasn't playing well.

His dad had called to him a couple of times, "Miles, play your game. Go after those guys!"

But he hesitated. He wasn't sure what the coach wanted from him. He took his shots when he got them, or he passed off. But he didn't want to push too hard and get accused of taking over the whole offense.

He did play tough defense.

He was playing tight on Johnson, a kid who was easy to guard. The player was a fair shooter, but he wasn't very quick. Miles was making life miserable for him.

Kenny was also back in the game. Soon after he returned, he rattled Higdon. Higdon needed to get rid of the ball. He looked right at Johnson before he passed the ball to him.

Miles saw the pass coming and broke in front. He picked the ball clean. He drove past Higdon, heading for the other hoop.

Harrison had a better angle than Higdon—and better speed. He cut toward Miles and then ran with him, step for step, down the court.

Miles thought he could take the ball all the way in.

He was ready to do his little hesitation, left-handed lay-up, when he thought maybe he shouldn't. Maybe that was "forcing up" a shot he shouldn't take. Maybe that was "showboating."

He backed off, suddenly, and looked around for a trailer. Higdon was still coming up behind him. But Jackie had run hard, and she was coming down the right side of the court.

Miles snapped a pass to her, but he was an instant late.

Higdon reached out and knocked the ball away. The ball flew out of bounds and the Lakers missed their chance for the lay-up.

Harlan tossed the ball in. Jackie took it to the top of the key and started a play. Josh missed a short jumper, and Harlan grabbed the rebound.

But he missed an easy shot, right by the basket. The Lakers had missed their chance.

The Clippers got the rebound and came back the other way. LeDuc took a pass in the corner, and she let fly with a three-pointer that hit the rim, bounced high, then dropped in.

The Clippers were ahead 25 to 23.

And that was the score at halftime.

Coach Donaldson paced and shouted, as usual. He asked Miles, "Didn't you come to play today? Is that why you're standing around out there?"

Miles was confused. What did this guy want from him?

"I don't know what you're thinking about, Harris. But you're letting your team down."

When Miles went back to the court, he didn't know what he was supposed to do.

He missed the first two shots he took, and the coach finally put him on the bench and put Stephanie Kadish in for him.

Strangely, the team actually started playing better after that. It wasn't that Stephanie played better. But everyone else seemed to do what they had to do.

Jackie ran the plays well, and Harlan made some great passes. Josh went hard to the boards. He and Harlan put in most of the Lakers' missed shots on second tries.

On defense, Jackie and Kenny had made up their minds that they weren't going to give up those long shots to the Clippers' guards.

The Clippers' long shots weren't going down very often. And their shooters usually only got one chance against the taller Lakers' rebounders.

By the early part of the fourth quarter, the score was 38 to 31. The Lakers were starting to pull away.

Miles could hardly believe what he was seeing. The team was better off without him.

The coach finally put Miles back in the game. And Miles tried hard to get something going. But the shots still weren't falling for him.

So he quit shooting. He worked hard on defense. He crashed the boards for the rebounds.

The Lakers ended up destroying the smaller Clippers in the fourth quarter.

By the end of the game, the score was 53 to 36.

And Angel Park had the win it needed.

But no one seemed exactly happy when it was all over. The Lakers knew they hadn't played well. The spark was gone, and no one knew what to do about it.

After the game, Miles rode his bike home with Kenny and Harlan.

"Don't worry," Kenny told Miles. "You just had an off day. That happens to everybody. I saw Michael Jordan on TV one time when he couldn't hit anything."

Harlan laughed. "Yeah, Miles, you can't expect to score as many points as a guy like *me*."

It was true. For the first time all season, someone besides Miles was the high scorer for the Lakers. With all those rebound shots, Harlan had scored the most points.

Miles laughed at Harlan. "Hey, man, you've come a long way this year. You played *great* today."

"You'll play great next time, Tip. You weren't bad today. You just weren't *hot*."

"Maybe it's good we've got a week off," Kenny said.

The three of them had stopped at a corner. They had to wait for a red light.

A boy from their school, a guy named Brent, was coming across the street. "Did you guys win today?" he asked.

"Yeah, we did," Harlan said.

"Jonathan says the Bulls already have the championship locked up."

"Yeah, that sounds like Swingle," Harlan said. "But his team has to beat the Warriors, and the Warriors are tough. If the Bulls lose, we'll end up in a tie—and then have a play-off."

"Jonathan says the Warriors are no problem."

"Yeah, well, Jonathan might be wrong."

After Brent walked on, Kenny said, "Harlan, don't forget, *we* have to beat the Rockets."

"We will," Harlan said.

Miles agreed. What he didn't expect was that the Bulls would lose. And he wasn't sure he wanted that to happen. The thought of playing those mouthy Bulls again worried him. He didn't know whether he could handle the stuff they might dish out.

Miles had never doubted himself so much in his whole life.

But the next Saturday morning, he and all his friends from the Lakers showed up to watch the Bulls and the Warriors play.

It was a battle, too.

It was tight all the way, and the crowd was really noisy. It was easy to see that the two teams didn't have a lot of love for each other.

The Lakers' players didn't cheer out loud for the Warriors, but they wanted, more than anyone in the gym, to see them win.

The Bulls led almost all the way.

But the Warriors came back. They got within a point as time was running out.

That's when Swingle messed up. He tried to dribble the time away, and he dribbled the ball off his foot and out of bounds.

The Warriors got a last shot, and they fed the ball to big Hausberg, under the basket. He laid the ball in and the Warriors won by one point.

So the Lakers were still alive!

Miles was happy, but he also felt the pressure come back. He would probably have to play those mouthy guys again. For now, the Lakers had to be sure they beat the Rockets.

★ 5 ★

Rock the Rockets

By the time the morning came for the Rockets game, Miles was tired of thinking. He made up his mind to play his own game. If the coach didn't like what he did, he could stick him on the bench again. That seemed to work out all right last time.

Just before Miles walked out to start the game, Derek Mahana yelled to him, "Hey, Miles, let's *rock* these guys!"

And Miles liked the sound of it. He thought about playing in his neighborhood—relaxed and confident.

The game had hardly begun before he was making things happen.

Watrous, a pretty good player, was

guarding Miles. But Miles made him look silly. He drove right past him.

Then Watrous started giving him more room. So Miles took the open long shots, and he made those.

He made the first four shots he took and the Lakers were up 8 to 2.

Big Santos had made things tough for Harlan earlier in the season. But Harlan had learned a lot since then. He was staying right with the guy, keeping the ball from him.

Watrous was the other big scorer for Paseo. But Miles stayed so tight he couldn't get a pass. When he did get the ball a couple of times, Miles wouldn't give him a chance to shoot.

By the end of the first quarter, Miles had another basket, and Jackie and Josh had each scored.

At the same time, the Rockets' offense was falling apart against the tough defense the Lakers were playing.

The score at the end of the quarter was 14 to 4.

Coach Donaldson had never been quite

so pleased. He actually told the players they were doing a good job. "Great defense!" he told them. "Just great. Miles, you took good shots. And you put 'em in the hole. Nice work."

But then he told Jackie, "Now don't start depending too much on Harris. Move the ball around."

That was fine with Miles—fair enough.

But as he walked back to the court, Watrous was staring at him. "Harris, you're not half as good as you think you are," he said.

Here we go again, Miles thought.

But he acted as though he hadn't even heard the guy. Miles had just scored ten points. That ought to answer anything Watrous had to say.

And yet, deep down, it really bugged Miles. Why couldn't the guy just play hard and forget all that stuff?

But it didn't stop.

Miles had the feeling that Watrous knew something. Maybe everyone in the league was talking. Maybe they were saying, "If you get in Harris's face and give him a hard time, he starts pressing too hard. He messes up."

Or maybe this guy was just jealous, like Korman.

Miles didn't know. But he knew he couldn't let it bother him.

The Lakers' offense worked well again in the second quarter. Everyone was getting a chance to shoot, and everyone seemed to have the hot hand.

The defense let down a little, maybe—especially as the substitutes played more. But the Lakers were steadily moving away. The score bulged to 27 to 12.

The Rockets just couldn't stay with the Lakers today.

Miles only took a couple of shots in the quarter. But he was open, and he knocked them down.

Watrous could hardly stand it.

He kept up the stupid talk. But Miles just kept his mouth closed. The only trouble with that was, Watrous seemed to be getting more frustrated all the time.

Finally he said, "Hey, Harris, I saw you blow that game against the Suns. You couldn't even make a foul shot when your team needed it. When the game's on the line, you choke up."

Miles said nothing.

Absolutely nothing.

But he was getting angry—no matter how much he told himself not to.

Still, he went hard to the hoop on his drives. He even did one of his hesitation lay-ups, and he made Watrous look stupid.

But he didn't say anything afterward. He just gave Watrous a look that said, "Take that, smart mouth."

Watrous shut up for the rest of the half.

And Miles felt that he was in control.

When the second half started, the coach took the whole first team out. He let the second team get some playing time together.

By now, the score was 35 to 16.

The second team held its own. The lead stayed about the same through the quarter.

And the kids on the bench—the first team players—were having fun. They shouted and whooped it up when their teammates scored. And they talked about going after the Bulls for the championship.

The Bulls would be playing the Clippers right after this game. No doubt, they would have no problem winning. So the season would end a tie.

The play-off game was becoming a sure thing.

The quarter ended with the score 38 to 20.

The coach put the first team back in. "All right. Now let's make this a tune-up for the championship," he said. "See if you can run that offense like a machine. And go after those kids on defense. Pretend you're playing the Bulls."

The Lakers cheered and shouted as though they were about to start the big game. The Rockets all looked across the court, surprised.

But the Lakers came out *hot*. And they played as though they were down ten points and had to make a big comeback.

Their defense was almost perfect. They played man-to-man, and they covered the Rockets like a pack of dogs.

Even the Rockets' first team would have had trouble, but some subs were in the lineup. They got frantic and started throwing the ball all over the place.

On offense, the Lakers were going hard, working to get open, setting good screens.

Harlan hit a spin-and-fire shot from the foul line. And then Jackie split the strings with a pull-up jumper from inside the paint.

When Miles got the ball, he faced Watrous, gave him a head fake, and then drove to the right. Watrous managed to cut him off at the baseline.

Miles spun and faked an off-balance left-handed hook shot. But instead, he shot a darting pass to Kenny, who had cut down the lane.

Kenny went up for the shot—but didn't shoot.

He flipped the ball, underhand, right back to Miles, who was moving in for a possible rebound.

Miles went up high and banged in the lay-up. But Watrous, caught out of position, tried to block him from behind.

The basket counted, and Miles was shooting a foul shot.

He lofted a perfect shot, and now the score was 48 to 22. The Lakers had a 10 to 2 run going.

Miles turned to run back up the court. But suddenly he felt his legs go out from under him. He was on his chest so quickly he hardly knew what had happened.

Then he realized. Someone had tripped him.

He jumped up to see Watrous running away. The guy had knocked a leg out from under him without the ref even noticing.

Miles was angry, but he told himself not to lose it. He ran hard and caught up with Watrous.

"What happened, hotshot, did you fall down?" Watrous said. He turned and grinned.

He had little teeth, like a rodent. Miles wanted to make him eat a couple of them. But instead, he said, "I'm going to make you look like a *fool* for that."

"Just try," Watrous said.

McCarty put up a shot that fell short. Josh got the rebound.

Miles had made up his mind. He was going to show this kid something—with the basketball, not his mouth.

He ran up the floor, then suddenly stopped. He cut back toward Jackie. "Toss me the ball," he said.

She hesitated, but then she did throw it

to him. Miles dribbled in an arc, not toward the hoop, but straight at Watrous.

As he approached Watrous, he slowed. But then—*bam*—he dribbled behind his back and cut to the left. Watrous chased him, but Miles did a spin move that left Watrous running clear past. Then he broke to the hoop, alone.

Miles jumped, as though he were going for a simple lay-up. Instead, he flipped the ball underhand, with twist on it.

The ball spun off the glass and into the basket.

When Miles came down, he turned and looked straight into Watrous's face. But he didn't say a word.

Watrous jumped up against Miles's chest, ready to fight.

Harlan stepped in close, and then shoved himself between the two.

"Hey, let's play ball," the referee yelled. Watrous gave it up, and ran back up the floor.

Miles took off after him. But when Jackie picked up a foul, the action stopped. Coach Donaldson used the chance to send Ben in for Miles.

Miles walked toward the bench with his

hands on his hips. He heard Watrous say, "Those guys are *all* like that. They think they're *so bad.*"

Miles spun around. But his coach was yelling, "Harris, get over here."

So Miles walked off the floor.

"Go back where you came from!" he heard one of the Rockets yell.

Miles dropped onto the bench. He felt completely alone.

"What's it going to take with you, Harris?" the coach asked. "Are you going to keep letting these kids get to you?"

"I didn't *say* anything. I just put some moves on the guy."

"You lost your temper." The coach walked over and stood in front of Miles. "You made the basket, but you forgot there was a team out there. The only thing you wanted to do was make the guy look bad."

Miles had heard enough. He jumped up and faced the coach. "That's right. That's *exactly* what I wanted to do. And he had it coming. You don't know what's been going on out there."

"I don't *care* what's going on. We're here

to win a basketball game—not to show people up."

"It's not basketball when guys are knocking you down and calling you names."

But the coach had moved in another step, and he was almost on top of Miles. "Quit your crying, Harris," he shouted into Miles's face. "You're not going to get any pity from me. Now sit down and be quiet."

Miles was furious. But he didn't want to be accused of "crying." So he did sit down. And for a while, he thought of all the things he wanted to tell the coach.

And yet, after he had sat on the bench for a couple of minutes, he knew the truth. Watrous had won. He had finally gotten under Miles's skin. And Miles had promised himself that wouldn't happen again.

The Lakers won the game, 57 to 23.

Yet Miles had the feeling that *he* had lost.

And so had the coach. There were things that shouldn't happen on a basketball court. And Coach Donaldson could do something about it if he really wanted to.

★ 6 ★

Friends

=========

A lot of the Lakers stuck around after the game to watch the Bulls and Clippers play. They didn't really expect the Clippers to knock off the Bulls. But . . . it was always possible.

Miles didn't stay.

He rode home alone on his bike. A little rain was falling, and it was cold. But he hardly noticed.

He felt the cold that was inside him.

When Miles got home, he got his basketball and went outside. Even with the wind, and the sprinkles of rain, it was what he wanted to do.

At first he took some simple shots. But gradually he got into the action.

He was soon driving to the hoop, making moves, juking and jumping, playing against no one—but playing like he always had, back in his old neighborhood.

It used to be, when he showed up at the playground, guys would start yelling, "Hey, Tip's here. We get Tip."

And the team who got him usually got the win, too.

He had been *somebody*. And no one hated him for being good. No one hated him at all.

Miles imagined himself slipping by a guard, driving past a big center, putting up his reverse lay-up.

"Game tied," he whispered to himself. "Tip gets the ball. He drives, fakes, goes up. And *bang*, he hits the jumper."

And he *did* hit the jumper.

In fact, he was hitting everything. The wind and rain didn't bother him at all.

He must have sunk seven or eight shots in a row before he finally tried a tricky lay-up that rolled off the hoop.

That's when he heard Kenny's voice. "Hey, we thought you were never going to miss."

Miles turned around and saw Kenny and

Harlan. They were standing at the front of his driveway. Miles had been so involved in his "game" that he hadn't noticed them.

Now they were walking toward him. Kenny said, "Well, the Bulls won."

That was no surprise.

Kenny and Harlan both had their jackets zipped to the top. "Aren't you cold?" Harlan asked.

"No."

"Miles, I don't blame you for showing Watrous up," Kenny said. "He was working on you the whole game."

"Tell the coach that." Miles chased after the ball.

"Hey, I can't tell the coach anything."

"No one can," Harlan added.

Miles was walking back. He had the ball under his arm, resting against his side.

"I gotta go in now," he said. "I'll see you guys later."

"Miles, the Bulls are going to try to get you mad—the same as today. You just can't let them bother you."

Miles kept walking. But when he got to his back door, he stopped and looked around. "Could you do that, Kenny?"

Kenny walked over to the back steps, and Harlan followed. "Miles," Kenny said, "I don't think those guys care anything at all about your race. It's just something they use to—"

"Kenny, you don't know what it's like. No one gives Mexican guys a hard time." He opened the door to go in.

"Miles, we've been through this before. You know I've had some stuff happen to me."

"Like what?"

Kenny tucked his hands into his jacket pockets. "Well, like—when I was about seven or eight, I went on a trip with my family. We were up by Fresno—in a little town. I guess a lot of farm workers from Mexico go up there to pick fruit and work in the fields. But we were just passing through, and we stopped at a little place to get something to eat."

"Kenny, what's this got to do with anything?"

"Just listen. This waitress walked up to us and said, 'I'm sorry, but I can't seat you.' My dad said, 'Why not?' The place was almost empty. But she just said, 'I'm sorry, sir.' So he said, 'You're *going* to be sorry when I report you.' And then she seemed to get the idea—like 'Oh, oh, this guy speaks good English.' And she told us to follow her to a table. But my dad said, 'No, thanks. I don't want to eat here,' and we left."

Now Miles got the point. He nodded.

"I didn't know what was going on until we got outside. I asked my dad, and he said, 'Kenny, I'm sorry you had to see that. But some people don't like the Mexican farm workers.' I still didn't get it. I said, 'We're not Mexican farm workers.' And he said, 'I know. But my family came to this country from Mexico. And some people don't like *any* Mexicans—even if they've lived here all their lives.' "

Miles could see it in Kenny's eyes, hear it in his voice. He *did* understand.

"That was the first time I knew that anybody felt that way. I got back in the car, and I stared out the window for about an hour. I didn't say a word. I just didn't know until then."

"I learned sooner than that," Miles said. "When I was little, my family went out to the beach in Santa Monica. We were walking along and a white woman said, 'I wish they wouldn't let those people on this beach. It's going to get so trashy.' When she first said it, I looked around to see who 'those people' were. And then I looked at her, and I knew. She said it loud, on purpose, so we would hear. And she was staring right at us."

Kenny didn't say anything, but the two looked at each other, and Miles could see that Kenny understood.

"I'm sorry stuff like that happens," Harlan said.

And Miles knew he meant it.

"I was older when I found out."

The voice had come out of the house—and it was a voice Miles could never mistake.

Coach Donaldson.

The coach stepped outside, and Mr. Harris followed. Miles was shocked to see the guy at his house.

The boys all stepped back, as though they thought the coach might start in on them— as usual. Miles walked down off the steps.

"When I found out, I was in junior high," the coach said. "I wanted to go out for basketball, but I didn't have decent shoes. And I couldn't afford any. I finally borrowed some from my cousin—but they were about three sizes too big and all full of holes. I showed up for tryouts, and all the boys made fun of me. I didn't care. I just wanted to make the team. And I made it, too. The coach even went out and bought me some shoes—out of his own pocket."

The coach hesitated and folded his arms across his chest. Miles thought it was a strange story. They guy had heard Kenny and Miles, but—as usual—he had missed the point.

"I was on the team," Coach Donaldson said, "but that didn't mean the team members were my friends. I was from the wrong side of town, and those guys wouldn't have one thing to do with me. They didn't mind if I helped them win games, but in the hallways at school, they wouldn't even speak to me. My clothes were too shabby. My house was down by the tracks. They couldn't hang around with a guy like that."

Everyone was silent.

Miles was stunned. Somehow it had never seemed to him that Coach Donaldson had ever been young—or that he had ever been anything but a hard-nosed basketball coach.

"I'll tell you how I reacted," the coach said. "I just stayed to myself. But I practiced basketball night and day. That was my way of getting back. By the time I was a senior in high school, I was the *star*. I still didn't have a lot of friends, but my teammates respected me for what I could do."

Miles was trying to think about all this. He was seeing the coach in a whole new way.

Finally Mr. Harris said, "I guess we all react in different ways to these things." He walked down off the steps and put his arm around Miles's shoulders. "But it's not easy when you're eleven years old, and you've got guys working you over—especially when they start making racial remarks."

"I know that," Coach Donaldson said. He came down off the steps too, and now the five formed a little circle. "But that's why he has to be tough. He's got to block all that stuff out—or they'll never stop riding him."

"He shouldn't have to put up with it. The referees should stop it. The coaches should."

"They try. But you can never stop it completely. I've pulled Miles out of the game every time I thought he was starting to lose his temper."

"He's got a *right* to lose his temper when kids start that stuff."

"Well, that's one way to look at it. But another way is to teach him to handle it. That's the only way I know to deal with that kind of stuff."

But the coach wasn't telling the whole story. And it was time to say something. "I don't think it's just guys like Korman and Watrous who are prejudiced," Miles said. "I think *you* are, too."

"I know that's what you think," the coach said. "Your dad and I were just in the house talking about that. But it's not true. I know I'm tough on you, but it has nothing to do with—"

"You had your mind made up about me right from the beginning. If I dribbled behind my back, I was showing off. If I beat a guy one-on-one, that wasn't *team* play."

"All right. I admit that. I'm from the old school, and I don't like that stuff. But I can see where the one-on-one stuff can work sometimes. I have no problem with that. What I *don't* like is showing off and putting guys down."

Mr. Harris said, "A good move isn't showing off. Black kids on playgrounds started dribbling between their legs—or behind their backs—but now every guard in the NBA uses those moves. And they make sense for a basic reason—they put a kid's body between the ball and the defender. That's one of the things you teach these kids."

"Well, I know," Coach Donaldson said. "But kids this age try that stuff and kick the ball away half the time."

"Miles doesn't," Kenny said.

"No. He doesn't. And I admit I've been slow to accept that."

The coach was sounding pretty good. But Miles wasn't sure he trusted him. Maybe he was just trying to please Miles's dad.

"Coach," he said, "you weren't fair to Jackie until we pushed you into letting her play. Was that because she's black?"

"No. Definitely not." The coach sounded sure of himself. But then his eyes dropped away from all the eyes that were watching his. "But it *was* because she's a girl."

Miles was surprised again.

"When I was growing up, girls just didn't play the game. It's been hard for me to accept the idea that a girl could go out there and lead a team of boys. But she's done it. And I've learned something about that, too."

Everyone seemed to think things over. It

was Harlan who finally said, "If we're going to beat the Bulls, we can't feel like our biggest enemy is our own coach. Sometimes you talk to us like you don't even like us."

The coach blew out his breath, and then shook his head. "Look, kids, that's the way my high school coach was. He was a good guy, but he was tough as nails. I guess that's been my idea of how it's supposed to be. And I probably won't change all that much. But I'm proud of you kids. We didn't start out with the best talent—and we had very little size—but we've got a chance to win the whole thing next week."

"And a lot of credit for that belongs to you," Mr. Harris said.

Miles had to admit that was true.

Maybe there was more that could be said, but Miles was feeling a whole lot better. He just didn't know how to say it. Then his hand came out. "Let's beat the Bulls," he said.

"Good idea," Coach Donaldson said.

Miles and the coach shook hands.

★ 7 ★

Time to Play

Miles thought he saw a difference in the coach that week. He still talked pretty tough, but some of the hardness seemed gone from his voice. He even laughed a couple of times.

Miles and Kenny and Harlan told the rest of the players about the conversation they had had with the coach. Everyone had trouble believing the man had said those things. But they also thought they saw a difference in him.

The big thing was, everyone was focused now on winning the game.

On Saturday morning, however, Miles realized that his problem hadn't really changed that much. He felt as though he had more people on his side, but he still had to keep control.

And this time it started before the game even got going. While Miles was warming up, the Bulls players—who went to school with him and were supposed to be his friends—started in on him.

"Hey, Miles," Jonathan Swingle yelled, "you can't beat us by yourself. You better try to pass once in a while."

"Don't listen to him," Kenny told Miles.

Miles was already telling himself the same thing.

But as it turned out, once the tipoff went up, the Bulls didn't have all that much to say. The fans, and the players on the bench, were making plenty of noise. But no one seemed to focus on Miles.

Maybe part of that was because the Bulls got off to a good start.

Eddie Boschi knocked the tip to Daynes, and he hustled into the forecourt and passed to Lakey. Lakey hit Boschi, who was breaking down the lane.

Harlan cut Boschi off, but Eddie kicked the ball right back to Lakey, who had gotten away from Josh. Lakey sank the jumper, and the Bulls broke out on top.

The Lakers came right back and set up a play.

Kenny passed to Harlan and then zipped down the lane. Harlan passed back to Kenny on a give-and-go play.

Kenny drove toward the basket but got stopped in the middle. He tried to go up with a shot.

Eddie got a hand on the ball, however, and knocked it away. Maria Tafoya picked up the loose ball, and she tossed it out to Daynes, who took off on a fast break.

He missed the shot, but Swingle trailed the play and snatched the rebound. He muscled the put-back shot up and in over Kenny.

The score was 4 to 0, just like that.

And it was 6 to 0 before Miles got his hands on the ball. Swingle was guarding him. No question, he had made up his mind to stop Miles.

Mrs. Taylor, the coach, had probably been getting him psyched all week to keep Miles from doing his usual damage.

But Miles drove straight at Swingle and forced him back. Then he pulled up and snapped off a beautiful arching jump shot.

Two points!

Miles heard Lakey say, "Jonathan, you can't give him that much room."

"Okay, okay," Jonathan said, and he sounded disgusted with himself.

Miles couldn't hold back a smile. Cover me close, and I'll drive on you, he told himself.

Daynes took a shot from outside that was long and off the glass. Harlan got up for the rebound and passed quickly out to Jackie.

Jackie passed ahead to Kenny. He took the ball straight down the middle of the floor. Miles was running on his left.

Kenny made Maria think he was going all the way. But then he shoveled the ball out to Miles.

Swingle was right with Miles.

Miles took a couple of slow dribbles, and then—*pow*—he took off. He got a step on Swingle and was gone. He laid the ball in, and the score was 6 to 4.

And that's how things stayed through the whole first quarter. The Bulls were tall, and they were good. They were going all out on defense.

But so were the Lakers.

Both teams were struggling to get clear shots off.

The only problem was, the Bulls were getting the edge on rebounds.

Boschi put back a couple of missed shots, and the Lakers were usually getting only one shot at the basket when they had the ball.

Still, the Lakers also had something going: Miles "Tip" Harris.

He was doing it all.

He could feel it within himself today. He wasn't showing off, wasn't putting anyone down. But he knew he was better—quicker, smarter—than Jonathan Swingle.

He could drive on the guy. He could fake him off his feet. And if Jonathan played it safe and stayed back a little, Miles could hit the jumper.

As the quarter was coming to an end, Jackie passed to Josh. Then she ran toward him and set a screen. Josh shook loose from Lakey and shot a jump shot from the foul line.

Miles saw the shot was off line. He charged at the hoop. Eddie and Harlan jumped at the same time. They knocked the ball away from each other.

As the ball looped in the air, Miles jumped. He caught the ball maybe ten feet from the basket. But without coming down, he controlled the ball and let go with a shot.

He used the glass, and the shot caromed right into the basket.

The shot tied the score, 14 to 14.

The crowd cheered. Even the Bulls' fans gave Miles a hand.

A few seconds later the buzzer sounded and the quarter was over.

Miles felt good. He had scored a lot of points. But he had also played tough defense and rebounded well, and he had made some good passes.

And it had really felt good when *all* the fans had given him a hand.

He turned to walk off the court. Behind him, he heard, "You're not going to keep scoring like that, Harris. I'm going to *stop* you."

He knew Swingle was just frustrated. But he wondered what that might turn into.

The coach substituted for Miles at the beginning of the second quarter. But only for a couple of minutes.

The Bulls scored six quick points to the Lakers' two. And the coach sent Miles back in.

Miles cut the four-point lead to one, just like that. He popped in a three pointer even though Swingle jumped high to try to block the shot.

But Swingle didn't like that.

"Don't look so cocky. You got lucky," he said.

Why couldn't they just play basketball?

At the other end of the court, Swingle cut off a screen, and got a pass in deep, close to the paint.

Miles slipped the screen and jumped. He may have touched the ball, but Swingle went up hard. He muscled the ball over Miles, and the shot went in.

"Nice shot," Miles said.

Swingle gave him a funny glance, as if to say, "Don't smart off with me."

But Miles wasn't being sarcastic. It *was* a nice shot, and Miles just wanted all the ugly talk to end.

The game turned a little ragged for a couple of minutes after that. Passes were getting away. Shots weren't dropping.

Miles even stumbled and got called for traveling.

The Bulls' players liked that.

Miles heard the usual "hotshot" stuff coming from the bench. He didn't pay too much attention, but it seemed dumb that they should enjoy his mistake so much. He had been ripping them, and they knew it.

As the first half was coming to a close, the score was staying very tight. For a while, one team would take a one-point lead and then the other. But then Maria picked off a long rebound and put a shot back up.

She sank the shot, and the Bulls went up by three, 29 to 26.

Jackie hustled down the court with the

ball. The seconds were ticking away, under thirty to go.

She suddenly turned on her speed, and drove down the middle. The defense closed in on her and she spun and shot a quick pass out to Miles.

He went up for a shot, but Swingle got up with him, his hands high in the air.

Miles didn't get off a very good shot. It banged off the glass and Boschi got the rebound.

"What's the matter, *star*?" Swingle hissed behind Miles's back.

But the Bulls still had a few seconds. Boschi passed to Maria and she looked down the floor to Swingle. She threw a long pass to him.

Miles darted in. Just as Swingle caught the ball, Miles reached in and knocked it out of his hands.

He slipped past Swingle and picked up the loose ball. Then he *shot* down the court.

And he was all alone.

Swingle ran after him, but he couldn't catch up.

Miles couldn't resist doing a little something extra with the lay-up. He could have gone straight to the hoop on the left, but he crossed under, and flipped up the reverse lay-up with his left hand.

He could have looked really silly if he had missed it.

But no way. The ball spun into the hoop.

The lead was cut to one, 29 to 28.

And the half was over.

But when Miles turned around, Swingle was staring him in the face. "You don't have to do that showoff stuff."

"Yeah, and you don't have to be a *jerk* either, Swingle."

"You bring it on yourself, Miles. You always have to—"

"Look, I wasn't showing off. It's just . . . show time. When you break away, that's what you do."

"Maybe where you come from. Not around here."

During halftime Miles thought about that. On the playground—back in his old neighborhood—guys liked that stuff. Even players on the other team would tell you when you made a hot move. What was so bad about that?

Miles didn't mind fitting in a little, but these guys could give him some room, too. He didn't mind cutting out a little of the hotdog stuff, if kids thought he was trying to put them down. But he wasn't going to change his style of play. No one asked Michael Jordan to stop making his moves!

★ 8 ★

Winner Takes All

Miles was heading back to the floor when he realized that the coach hadn't jumped all over the team during halftime. He had talked about their mistakes—plenty—but he hadn't sounded angry.

Now he called Miles over. "Harris," he said, "that Swingle kid probably just got his ears burned. He's going to try harder to stop you. And if he can't, expect to hear some trash. But it's all on the line now. You can't let him mess you up."

"Okay. I know. I won't let him get to me."

But it didn't take long to see that the coach was right.

Swingle was fired up.

Besides that, the guy was getting help. The

Bulls had gone into a zone, and they were cheating Maria off on Miles, daring the rest of the team to do the scoring.

Jackie took the dare, and she started going to the other players. But things didn't work very well. All during the third quarter, Miles rarely got his hands on the ball.

And the other players were struggling with the bigger, taller defensive players. Boschi was staying really tough on Harlan. And the zone was jamming up the middle.

Outside shots were open, but Kenny and Jackie both seemed tight. They hit some— but not as many as they needed to.

And most of the rebounds were going to the Bulls.

The Bulls began to build a lead.

Subs for both teams played for a while, and neither team looked all that great. But by the time the quarter was over, the Bulls were ahead, 39 to 33.

And now Swingle thought he had room to brag. "I guess I shut *you* down," he said.

Miles thought about saying, "Yeah—with some help." But he didn't. He trotted to the side of the court.

He could see that Coach Donaldson was

upset. "Don't you guys want to win this thing?" he asked them.

"Yeah, we do," some of them said.

"Well, you don't act like it."

Miles couldn't have tried any harder. He didn't think anyone on the team could have.

"We're playing hard," he said, under his breath.

"What's that, Harris?"

"I said we *are* playing hard."

Coach Donaldson stepped closer, and pointed a finger at Miles. But just as suddenly he caught himself. He stepped back and thought for a moment. "Okay. Okay. You're playing hard. But you're not playing *loose* and . . ." He stopped and thought again. "Well, I don't mean loose . . . exactly."

But he smiled at himself.

And everyone else smiled too. Coach Donaldson had actually admitted that "running the offense" wasn't everything.

But the smile was gone, quickly. "What's going wrong out there?" he asked.

"They're packing the middle, taking away our cuts," Jackie said. "And they're doubling on Miles."

"All right. We can just—"

"Coach?" Jackie said.

"Yeah."

"Why don't we clear out for Miles, and overload their zone?"

"You can't clear out when they're doubling on him."

"It will put four people on one side of the zone—with three to cover. Or else they'll stop doubling Miles. Maria won't be able to sag off. She'll have to go one way or the other."

The coach was nodding, listening to Jackie. "Okay. Let's try it," he said.

"Let's go after 'em *hard* on defense, too!" Josh said. And Miles saw the excitement come back into all the players' faces.

The Lakers ran back to the floor.

Jackie brought the ball in, and the offense cleared out, leaving Miles alone on the right side. Swingle stayed with Miles, but Maria played it halfway, not sure what to do.

Jackie passed to Miles and then cleared to the left with the others.

Maria ran straight to Miles, and for a moment, Miles looked trapped.

But he faked left, dribbled right, and then cut between the two defenders. Both tried to stay with him, but Miles suddenly pulled up.

Just then Harlan broke to the hoop, ahead of Boschi, who was caught trying to cover two people in his zone.

Miles hit Harlan, and Harlan laid the ball in.

At the other end of the floor, Lakey tried a drive, but Josh had him blocked. Lakey got called for an offensive foul.

The Lakers came right back and cleared out again.

Miles took the pass. At the same instant, Maria charged toward him. Miles lofted a loop pass over her head to Kenny, who was all alone.

Kenny fired a quick jumper that went down.

Now the Lakers were only behind by two, 39 to 37.

The Bulls got the ball to Boschi underneath the basket the next time down the floor. Harlan worked hard to stop him, but Boschi got the shot off. And it went in.

The Lakers hustled back fast. Miles caught the pass, faked a move, and then went straight up with a jump shot. He stung the strings for another two.

Miles was feeling it now. He was *hot*.

The lead was at two again.

Miles ran back up the floor, yelling to his teammates. He heard Swingle say something, but he paid no attention. He heard a lot of noise from the Bulls' bench, too, but it was just that—noise. He let the words go right on by.

He knew those guys were starting to feel some fear. The Lakers were on a roll.

The defense had really come alive.

Jackie swarmed all over Daynes. He stopped his dribble, and then he had to get rid of the ball. But he let fly with a high pass over Maria's head, and the ball went out of bounds.

Lakers' ball.

Back they came. This time they cleared out, but Jackie only faked the pass. When Maria took the fake and cut toward Miles, Jackie broke down the middle.

Boschi jumped into Jackie's path. Jackie bounced a pass to Miles, who was breaking for the hoop. He took the ball in stride, dribbled once, and soared through the air.

Boschi went up for the block, but Miles sailed under his arm, delayed his shot, and flipped it up and under the basket. The ball had perfect spin on it, and it twisted off the glass and into the net.

The score was tied, 41 to 41.

The Bulls called time out.

Mrs. Taylor was a good coach. She was waving for her team to hurry over. Miles knew some sort of change in the defense would be coming.

As the Lakers ran off the floor, their fans were all standing up, cheering like crazy.

"We're going to win this thing," Mr. Harris was shouting.

"Okay, good," Coach Donaldson said. "I suspect they'll be switching back to a man-to-man defense. Let's keep clearing out for now. But Miles, look for the open players. Don't try to do it alone."

"All right," Miles said, and he meant it.

The Lakers soon learned that the coach was right. The Bulls had gone to a man-to-man, and Swingle had fire in his eyes.

But the first time Miles got the ball, he juked Swingle to the left and drove right.

Boschi came at him, so Miles slipped a bounce to Harlan, underneath.

Bingo! Two points.

The Lakers were finally on top, and it seemed that there was no stopping them.

But the Bulls were tough. And they kept battling.

Neither team could mount a lead. Miles kept scoring, or passing off for scores. But the Bulls were coming through, too.

And then the defenses seemed to take over. For a while neither team could score.

With just under a minute left, Maria stole a pass and broke free on a fast break. She passed off to Swingle and he scored. The Bulls were up by one point, 48 to 47.

Swingle turned and growled at Miles. "We've got you now, hot shot. You're not scoring on *me* again."

But Miles got a pass from Kenny and then put a spin move on Swingle. This time he cut left and got free.

He went up for the jumper, and it felt good. But it hit just a little hard off the back of the rim and popped out.

Lakey grabbed the rebound.

Now the Bulls had the lead and the ball . . . with time running out.

"You can't do it when you *have* to, Harris," Swingle yelled. "You choke every time."

But Miles was thinking about getting the ball.

He jumped in with Jackie and tried to trap Daynes. But Daynes got a pass off to Maria.

Miles chased her down. She was trying to dribble and use up time.

Miles knew he might have to foul, but he didn't want to. He got right in her face, but he didn't reach in. She stopped her dribble, and the Lakers were covering well. She couldn't find anyone to pass to.

Finally she tried to feed Daynes, but Jackie was right there. She leaped in and stole the pass.

She flipped the ball back to Miles, but the Bulls had taken off very quickly. The fast break wasn't there.

Miles dribbled the ball hard up the floor. He knew the time was almost gone.

He slowed, looked things over, then broke hard for the basket again. In the paint he faked a pass, and then took the ball to the hoop himself.

Swingle almost took his head off. Miles ended up on the floor, flat on his back. For a moment, his vision was filled with little floating lights.

The ref was yelling, "Intentional foul. Two shots."

Miles got up. He knew the game was in his hands now.

He walked to the line.

He couldn't help thinking back to the last time he had come to the line with a game to win or lose.

And now the shouting had gone crazy.

His own fans were cheering for him, telling him he could do it. But the Bulls were going crazy. "Choke, choke," some of them were chanting. "Choke like you did before."

But Miles smiled. This was going to be sweet. He knew he wouldn't miss this time.

When the first shot hit the net, the Bulls suddenly fell silent for a moment. And then they started screaming again.

But Miles was still smiling.

He bounced the ball, brought it high— the way he had done a thousand times before.

Lift and . . . *release*.

Miles knew it was in the hoop.

And when the ball hit the bottom of the net, the Lakers' fans went wild.

Four seconds had to tick away, and the Bulls got off a desperation shot from mid-court.

But the game was over.

And the Lakers—the short guys—were the champions.

The champions!

Miles got piled on, and he ended up so deep under arms and legs, that he just lay on the floor and laughed.

When he finally got up, he slapped hands with everyone he could. Then he grabbed Kenny and Harlan and threw his arms around both of them at the same time. All three of them jumped up and down together.

It was about then that Miles heard Mrs. Taylor, the Bulls' coach. "Congratulations, Coach," she said to Mr. Donaldson. "You outsmarted us in the fourth quarter."

Coach Donaldson grabbed Jackie and pulled her over. "Say that again, Coach," he said. "What we did was Jackie's idea."

Jackie grinned when she heard Coach Taylor repeat what she had said.

And this time Mrs. Taylor added, "You could only make it work with a player like Miles. I wish I had had *him* all season."

She turned to Miles. "Young man, you're the best player your age I've ever seen. You'll be playing in the NBA someday. And I'm going to pay to watch you."

"I believe that, too," Coach Donaldson said. "And I'll tell you something else. These kids have taught me some things—and it hasn't all been about basketball."

The Lakers got their trophies after that. And Mr. Harris offered to take the whole team out for banana splits.

At the ice cream parlor, Coach Donaldson actually cracked a joke. And then laughed.

What a day!

Miles felt good. He still missed his old neighborhood—and he thought he always would.

But he could make it here. He knew he could.

Eleventh Game Scores:

San Lorenzo Suns	50	Angel Park Lakers	49
Blue Springs Warriors	52	Paseo Rockets	32
Angel Park Bulls	40	Santa Rita Jazz	28
Cactus Hills Clippers	bye		

Twelfth Game Scores:

Angel Park Lakers	53	Cactus Hills Clippers	36
Angel Park Bulls	46	Paseo Rockets	33
San Lorenzo Suns	47	Blue Springs Warriors	44
Santa Rita Jazz	bye		

Thirteenth Game Scores:

San Lorenzo Suns	37	Santa Rita Jazz	35
Cactus Hills Clippers	28	Paseo Rockets	22
Blue Springs Warriors	45	Angel Park Bulls	44
Angel Park Lakers	bye		

Fourteenth Game Scores:

Angel Park Lakers	57	Paseo Rockets	23
Blue Springs Warriors	43	Santa Rita Jazz	40
Angel Park Bulls	50	Cactus Hills Clippers	27
San Lorenzo Suns	bye		

Final League Standings

Angel Park Bulls	9–3
Angel Park Lakers	9–3
Blue Springs Warriors	8–4
San Lorenzo Suns	6–6
Santa Rita Jazz	6–6
Paseo Rockets	3–9
Cactus Hills Clippers	1–11

Play-off Game for League Championship

Angel Park Lakers	49	Angel Park Bulls	48

Passing

Nothing is more important to a team's offense than good passing. Smart, sharp passing can set up easy baskets. Sloppy passing causes turnovers and loss of offensive momentum. Good passing can be developed with practice. Passing is not as easy as it looks. It requires split-second timing, excellent judgment, and court awareness, that is, knowing where teammates are on the floor. The *fast break* is an exciting and effective offensive play that relies on all three. And practice, of course. Lots and lots of practice.

Smart Passing Checklist

Before passing
  Know where your teammates are
  Use pivot to buy time
  Don't broadcast the pass

When passing
  Use two hands
  Step toward receiver
  Snap wrists and fingers outward
  Pass to the side of the receiver
    opposite the defender

When catching a pass
  Never turn back to ball handler
  Always give passer a target hand
  Move to the pass
  Keep eyes on the ball

The Weave Drill

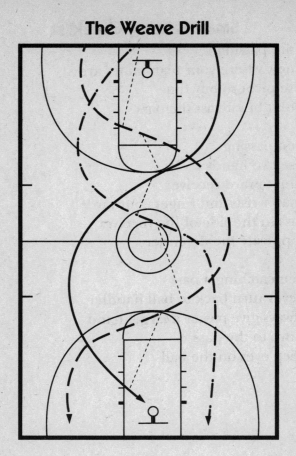

The passers are represented by the solid or broken lines. Passes are the small dotted lines. Each player passes the ball to the player in front of him and then cuts behind that player, running quickly upcourt to receive a pass from the third player, and so on.

Three-Lane Fast Break

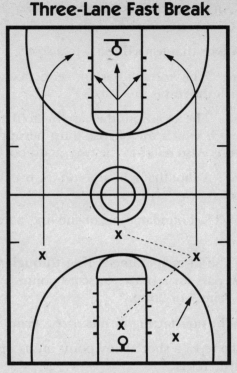

This play starts with the defensive rebound. The rebounder passes to outlet (usually a guard) on the sideline. The outlet passes to midcourt player. Two wide players streak up the sideline, and all three angle for the hoop. If there are no openings, a player following behind the middle dribbler can catch a "trailer" pass for an easy layup. (He's also in good position for a rebound if one of the lead players misses a shot.)

Glossary

airball An embarrassing shot that falls far short of the basket.

assist A pass that leads directly to a score.

backboard The rectangular or semicircular surface onto which the rim is mounted.

backcourt The area from the baseline to the midcourt line through which the offense must advance the ball after a score. Also refers to the two guard positions.

bank shot A shot that rebounds off the backboard into the hoop.

baseline The boundary line, or end line, at each end of the floor.

basket The 18-inch-diameter ring through which the ball must pass for a player to score points. Also called "hoop," "rim," or "iron."

bench The nonstarting members of a team.

block To repel a shot at any point on its upward arc. Also called "reject."

box out To square the body toward the basket in an effort to screen an opponent from getting a rebound. Also called "block out."

brick A low-arc shot that bangs clumsily off the rim. Taking terrible shots is called "throwing up bricks."

center The middle position in a three-player front line, usually the tallest member of the team.

charge A foul on a ball handler for running into a stationary defensive player who has established position.

clear out To free, or isolate, a ball handler to go one-on-one with a defender by rotating offensive players to the opposite side of the floor.

crash the boards To hustle for rebounds coming off the backboard.

cut A quick move by a player without the ball toward the basket for a possible pass.

double dribble An infraction in which a ball handler dribbles with both hands simultaneously or resumes a dribble after having stopped.

double-team Two players defending one opponent, also called "trapping."

downtown A shot taken far away from the basket.

drive To dribble hard toward the basket for a close shot at the goal.

fake Any move by a ball handler to deceive a defender into an off-balance position, such as a "head fake" or "pump fake."

fast break A hustling transition offense in which players move quickly upcourt before opponents can fall back on defense.

forward Either of the two outside positions in a three-player front line.

foul Illegal contact or unsportsmanlike conduct that may result in either a change of possession or a free throw for the player fouled.

free throw An undefended shot at the basket from a distance of 15 feet from the end line, awarded to a player who has been fouled.

free throw lane The 12-foot-wide rectangular area inside the free throw lines. Also called the "lane," "underneath," or the "paint."

give and go   A maneuver in which a player passes to a teammate, cuts to the basket, and looks for a quick return pass.

guard   Either of the two backcourt positions. A point guard usually calls plays and brings the ball upcourt; the off guard is often the team's best shooter.

hail mary   A desperation shot at the basket.

held ball   When opposing players have equal possession of the ball, resulting in a "jump ball." Instead of jumping, however, most teams today alternate possession as indicated by the possession arrow.

inbound   To bring the ball into play after a score, turnover, or other stoppage of play.

jump ball   The play that begins the game wherein a ball is tossed into the air above and between two opposing players by the referee.

key   The area that includes the free throw lane and free throw circle.

man-to-man defense   A method of defense in which each member of the defensive team is designated to guard a particular member of the offensive team.

midcourt line   The boundary that divides the playing surface into two equal halves, also called the "ten-second line."

outlet pass   A transition pass from a rebounder to a teammate usually positioned at or near either sideline.

pivot   The act of keeping one foot in place while holding the ball and moving the other foot one step in any direction.

point   A position in the front court, usually at the top of the key. A point guard might "pull up" here to signal a play.

post   The position the center plays on offense. In a "high post," the center plays near the top of the free throw circle. In a "low post," the center plays near the basket.

press   An aggressive type of defense in which players guard opponents very closely, designed to induce an opponent into committing a turnover.

rainbow   A pretty outside shot with a very high arc, as opposed to an airball.

screen   An offensive play in which a teammate, by establishing position, blocks a defender from guarding the ball handler, leaving him open for an uncontested shot. Also called a "pick."

shot   An aimed throw of the ball at the hoop. Familiar shots are the "jump shot," the "lay-up," the "hook shot," the "slam dunk," the "fadeaway jumper," and the "three-point shot."

showtime   Fast-paced and flashy style of play.

switch   A maneuver in which two teammates on defense shift assignments so that each guards the opponent usually guarded by the other.

ten seconds   The amount of time an offensive team has to inbound the ball from the baseline past the midcourt—or "ten-second"—line. A violation results in change of possession.

three-seconds violation   An infraction in which an offensive player remains inside the free throw lane for more than the permitted three seconds at a time.

tip-in   A field goal made when a player taps the ball in after a missed field goal attempt.

trailer   A player who follows closely, or "trails," a ball handler driving to the basket, either to rebound or to receive a quick pass for a basket.

transition   The act of switching from defense to offense, and vice versa.

travel   An infraction in which a ball handler takes more than two steps without dribbling or passing, resulting in a turnover. Also called "walk."

turnover   The loss of possession of the ball to the opposing team, through mistakes or infractions of the rules.

wings   The areas just below the free throw line and to the sides of the lane. Often the best point to begin an offensive attack.

zone defense   A method of defense in which each member of the defensive team guards a specified portion, or "zone," of the playing area.